For Simon, Alison and Laura
– A.H.B.

For Maxim and Olivia
– E.H.

LITTLE TIGER PRESS
An imprint of Magi Publications, London
www.littletigerpress.com
First published in Great Britain 1998
Text © 1998 A. H. Benjamin
Illustrations © 1998 Elisabeth Holstien
A. H. Benjamin and Elisabeth Holstien have asserted their
rights to be identified as the author and illustrator of this
work under the Copyright, Designs and Patents Act, 1988.
Printed in Belgium • ISBN 1 85430 572 7
1 3 5 7 9 10 8 6 4 2

A DUCK SO SMALL

by A. H. Benjamin

Pictures by Elisabeth Holstien

LITTLE TIGER PRESS

Duffle was a very small duck,
and all the other ducks laughed at him
because of his size.

"A duck so small can do nothing at all!"
they jeered.

I may be small, thought Duffle sadly,
but there must be *something* I can do.
He wondered what it could be.

Duffle looked around and noticed
Kingfisher perched on a reed. He was
just about to say hello when . . .

Kingfisher suddenly took off and dived,
straight as an arrow, into the water.
Kingfisher is small, thought Duffle, but he
dives well. Perhaps I could do that, too.

and came down again
like a falling rock.

"Look what I can do!"
Duffle called out to the
other ducks. He flew high
into the air . . .

Duffle hit the water and did a reverse belly flop.

"Ha-ha, what did we say," cried the other ducks. "A duck so small can do nothing at all!"

Poor Duffle felt very foolish.
He climbed out onto the
riverbank and wondered
what to do next.

Duffle saw Heron
standing perfectly still on
one leg in the shallow
water. What good balance
she has, thought Duffle.
Perhaps I could do that, too.

"Look what I can do!"
Duffle called as he stood
on one leg with his wings
spread out.

He wobbled this
way and that and . . .

landed flat on his beak.

"Ha-ha, what did we say," laughed the other
ducks. "A duck so small can do nothing at all!"

Duffle crept into the shade of a nearby tree
so the others wouldn't see him blush. He heard
a *tap, tap, tap* above his head.

Looking up, Duffle saw Woodpecker
making a hole in the trunk. What a strong beak
he has, thought the little duck. Perhaps I could
bore a hole, too.

"Look what I can do!" Duffle called out to the
other ducks. He flew up into the tree and perched on
a thick branch. *Peck, peck, peck,* he chipped at the wood.
"Oops," he cried as he lost his balance. Duffle
toppled from the branch and . . .

fell to the ground.

"Ha-ha, what did we say," cackled the other
ducks. "A duck so small can do nothing at all!"

All the other ducks were paddling and
splashing in the river, but poor Duffle decided
to hide in the rushes until they left. That way he
wouldn't have to listen to their teasing.

I'm not good at anything.
I'm just a small useless duck,
he thought. And a tear rolled
down his beak.

For a long time Duffle
heard the other ducks
quacking with laughter.
It seemed as though they
would never leave.

Then he listened again,
and they weren't laughing
anymore.

They were quacking in alarm!

Duffle paddled over to see what all the fuss
was about. The other ducks were crowded around
a tiny hole in the riverbank where a duckling had
gotten stuck.

"Oh, please get him out," begged the duckling's mother.

"We will," said the other ducks, but it was no use. They were just too big to squeeze into the hole.

All except for Duffle.
"Let *me* try," he said, and because
he was so small, he was able to reach
right in.

It didn't take him long
to rescue the trapped
duckling.

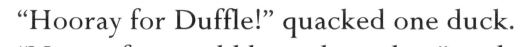

"Hooray for Duffle!" quacked one duck.
"None of us could have done that," said another.
"A duck so small *can* do something after all!"
cried a third.

"Oh, it was nothing," blushed Duffle.
But he knew it *was* something, and after that
the other ducks never made fun of him again.